Tiggers Hate to Lose

Disney's
Winnie the Pooh First Readers

DISNEP'S

A Winnie the Pooh First Reader

Tiggers Hate
to Lose

Isabel Gaines

ILLUSTRATED BY Francesc Rigol

DISNEP
PRESS

NEW YORK

First Edition

3 5 7 9 10 8 6 4 2

Library of Congress Catalog Card Number: 98-86080

ISBN: 0-7868-4266-0 (paperback)

For more Disney Press fun, visit www.DisneyBooks.com

Tiggers Hate to Lose

One fine spring day,
while bouncing beside the stream,
Tigger found Pooh and his friends
standing on the bridge.

They were all staring into the water.

"What are you doing?" Tigger asked.

"We're playing Pooh Sticks," said Pooh.

"Tiggers love Pooh Sticks!" said Tigger.

"What's Pooh Sticks?"

"It's a game," said Pooh.

"Get some sticks,

and you can play, too."

Tigger found some sticks

and bounced back to the bridge.

"The first stick to pass

under the bridge wins,"

explained Rabbit.

"On your mark, get set . . . go!"

Pooh, Piglet, Rabbit,
Roo, and Eeyore
threw their sticks
into the water.

Tigger decided to watch once
before trying it himself.

Then they all raced

to the other side

of the bridge

to see who won.

"I can see mine!" Roo shouted.

"I win!"

But just as he said the words,

Roo's "stick" spread its wings

and flew up

to join the other dragonflies.

"Can you see yours, Pooh?" Piglet asked.

"No," Pooh replied.

"I expect my stick is stuck."

"Look," Rabbit cried.

"There's Eeyore's stick!"

"Oh, joy," muttered Eeyore.

"I won."

"Step aside," Tigger said.

"Tiggers are great at Pooh Sticks."

Everyone moved over

so Tigger could play, too.

Once again, Rabbit gave the signal,

"On your mark, get set . . . go!"

They tossed their sticks

off the bridge . . .

20

. . . then raced to the other side.

Tigger shouted, "Did I win?"

"Nope," mumbled Eeyore. "I did."

"Oh," said Tigger, frowning.

"Well, I was just warming up.

Let's play again."

They played again,

and just like before,

Eeyore's stick sailed past the others.

"Tiggers don't like losing,"

grumbled Tigger.

"Let's play again."

Eeyore won the next game, too.

"Ooo, goody," Eeyore said.

"I've won four times in a row."

Eeyore won the next time,

and the next time,

and the time after that, too.

"I just can't lose," muttered Eeyore.

Tigger stamped his foot.

"Let's play again," he said.

"Tiggers *hate* to lose."

During the next game,

at the very last moment,

Eeyore's stick

squeaked by Tigger's.

Tigger threw down his sticks.

"Tiggers don't like Pooh Sticks!"

he cried.

Tigger walked away
with his head down
and no bounce at all.

"I'll tell you my secret,"

Eeyore called.

"You have to drop your stick

in a twitchy sort of way."

Tigger bounced back

to the bridge.

This time when he

dropped his stick,

Tigger made sure to twitch.

And this time,

Tigger's stick won!

Tigger was so happy,

he began bouncing again.

And he bounced right into Eeyore.

Can you match the words with the pictures?

stick

bridge

dragonfly

Tigger

Eeyore

Fill in the missing letters.

_ater

R_bbit

Pig_et

th_ew

foo_

Join the Pooh Friendship Club!

A wonder-filled year of friendly activities and interactive fun for your child!

The fun starts with:
- Clubhouse play kit
- Exclusive club T-shirt
- The first issue of "Pooh News"
- Toys, stickers and gifts from Pooh

The fun goes on with:
- Quarterly issues of "Pooh News" each with special surprises
- Birthday and Friendship Day cards from Pooh
- And more!

Join now and also get a colorful, collectible Pooh art print

Yearly membership costs just $25 plus 15 Hunny Pot Points. (Look for Hunny Pot Points on Pooh products.)

To join, send check or money order and Hunny Pot Points to:

Pooh Friendship Club
P.O. Box 1723
Minneapolis, MN 55440-1723

Please include the following information: Parent name, child name, complete address, phone number, sex (M/F), child's birthday, and child's T-shirt size (S, M, L)
(CA and MN residents add applicable sales tax.)

Call toll-free for more information
1-888-FRNDCLB

Fun for kids ages 3-8!

Help your child learn MATH and READING with a computer and a silly old bear.

Disney's Learning Series on CD-ROM

Put your child on the path to success in the 100 Acre Wood, where Pooh and his friends make learning math and reading fun. Disney's Ready for Math with Pooh helps kids learn all the important basics, including patterns, sequencing, counting, and beginning addition & subtraction. In Disney's Ready to Read with Pooh, kids learn all the fundamentals including the alphabet, phonics, and spelling simple words. Filled with engaging activities and rich learning environments, the 100 Acre Wood is a delightful world for your child to explore over and over. Discover the magic of learning with Pooh.

 NEW! Disney's Learning Series

Once Again The Magic Of Disney Begins With a Mouse

DISNEP INTER ACTIVE

Wonderfully Whimsical Ways To Bring Winnie The Pooh Into Your Child's Life.

Pooh FRIENDSHIP

Pooh and the gang help children learn about liking each other for who they are in 5 charming volumes about what it means to be a friend.

Pooh STORYBOOK CLASSICS

These 4 enchanting volumes let you share the original A.A. Milne stories — first shown in theaters — you so fondly remember from your own childhood.

Pooh PLAYTIME

Children can't help but play and pretend with Pooh and his friends in 5 playful volumes that celebrate the joys of being young.

Pooh LEARNING

Pooh and his pals help children discover sharing and caring in 5 loving volumes about growing up.

FREE*
Flash Cards Attached!
A Different Set With Each *Pooh Learning* Video!
* With purchase, while supplies last.